CW00857400

Coping Crew
Book #3

A Bat Afraid of the Dark

Written by: Stacey Lantagne | Illustrated by: Lynne Lillge

Italic Illustrator Shop

A Bat Afraid of the Dark
Coping Crew Book #3

Written by Stacey Lantagne
Illustrated by Lynne Lillge

Copyright © 2022 by Stacey Lantagne, Chelsey Lynne Lillge, and
Italic Illustrator Shop

Distributed in partnership with
Mythic North Press, LLC

All rights reserved, including the right to reproduce this book or portions thereof in any form.

https://www.italicillustratorshop.com/
https://www.craftersoncentral.com/

ISBN: 978-1-954177-26-0

Dedication

Readers who have now enjoyed the first 2 books of our Coping Crew Series have by now seen that every book dedication will always be dedicated to my family. This includes my husband, three children, mother and grandson, Ezra. I also dedicate and thank each of my books to my illustrator. Without her these books would have never been brought to life and for that I owe her a debt of gratitude. This book is of course dedicated to all of those same special people but I would also like to dedicate this to all healthcare workers, social workers, teachers and mentors for children. It is my hope that the Coping Crew Series can help not only to bring a smile or entertain your students or patients but to also open the door and pave the way for healthy and safe discussions about phobias, anxieties or fears to take place. I believe that starting conversations about mental health early in life is incredibly important. I appreciate each of you and all of your continued efforts. In closing, I of course thank each of my readers and hope that you enjoy this third book in our series.

You are not alone...
You have us.

Book #4

Book #1

Book #2

Book #5

Betty the bat had a problem you see
She was scared of the dark
unlike you and me.

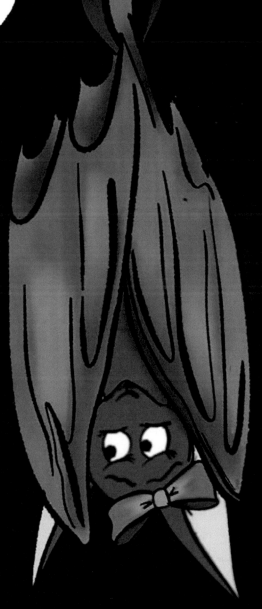

Betty was alone all day.
She really got bored.
She wished she slept too
When the other bats snored.

When the lights all went out
in the city and in town.
Betty the bat
would find a place to lie down.

One night a big cloud
Covered the sky.

She didn't feel dizzy.
Her body didn't shake.
Even though during the night,
She wasn't usually awake.

The next day she slept.
She woke up at night.

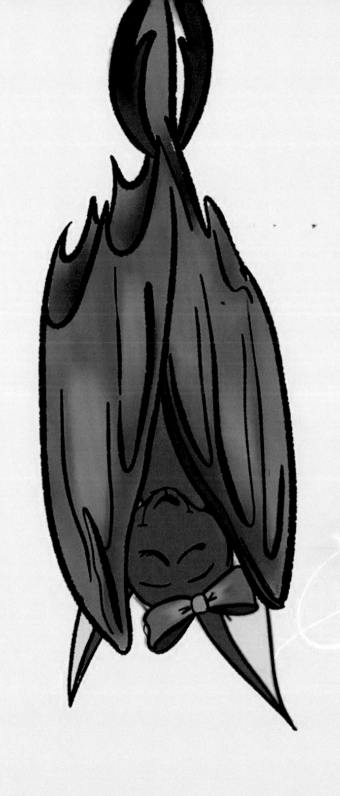

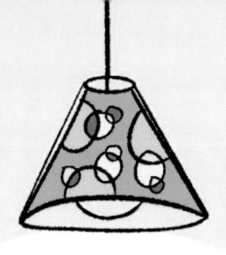

Betty felt happy.
Betty felt pride.
Betty felt relaxed now
On the inside.

Hi Readers!

Thank you for purchasing this book. I hope that you have enjoyed it and that you carry it along with you on trips in the car.
Your animal friends in this book would love to join you at school or daycare. They would love to go to the beach or the library.
Perhaps they could even keep you company when you are sick or before bed at night.

My name is *Stacey*. Can you think of other words that start with the

"*S*" sound?

What kind of animals start with the "*S*" sound?

I am the author of this book. This means that I came up with the words that either you or someone else read on the pages.
I have always wanted to write a book. I spend a lot of time in libraries with my large English Mastiff dog named Thor. Thor and I do pet therapy with kids and adults of all ages.

Some of our favorite books to hear are ones that rhyme like this book does.

In the past I have had numerous phobias and anxieties in my life.
Sometimes it can be hard to get over a fear.
I have had to learn different techniques and tricks to help me conquer my fears.
It is because of these phobias that I felt inspired to write this book. I want you all to know that you, too, can overcome obstacles and feel proud of yourselves when you achieve them.
Please do not ever feel alone in your fears or afraid to talk to someone about them.
There are so many wonderful tricks to help you.

I grew up a Yooper.
Do you know what that means? It means that I lived in the Upper Peninsula of Michigan (U.P.).
We have four beautiful seasons in the U.P. but our longest season is definitely winter. Do you get snow where you are from?
Can you find the U.P. on a map?

I no longer live in Michigan though. Now I live just across the border in the state of Wisconsin.
My husband and I own an art studio called Crafters on Central.
If you are ever traveling to Wisconsin, we hope that you can stop in to see our studio and get creative with a new art project.
We have a lot of fun things for a variety of ages.
We even have a splatter space that people can get REALLY messy in.
If you liked this book we hope that you get to meet other friends in our Coping Crew series.
Hopefully you can collect them all and that these characters become your friends just like I can be!
Choose to shine in all that you do!

Stacey

Lightning Source UK Ltd.
Milton Keynes UK
UKRC030207210922
408970UK00001BB/6